David McCheever's 29 DOGS

MARGARET HOLT

Illustrated by Walter Lorraine

Houghton Mifflin Company Boston / 1 9 6 3 / The Riverside Press Cambridge

to Philip, Paul, and Peter

David McCheever's family
had just moved into a new house.

David's mother asked him
to go to the store for her.

"I wish I had a friend,"
said David. "I wish
someone here knew me."
"You'll have lots of friends
when you go to school in September,"
his mother answered.

Then David set out for the store.
He said the list of things
that his mother wanted over and over
to himself.

"I would like hamburger,
and hot dogs, and beefsteak for three,
please," David said to the man
who sold the meat at the supermarket.

The man gave him the three kinds
of meat. Each of them was wrapped
in brown paper.

Then David found the bread
and the butter and walked
to the counter to pay for his things.
The girl at the counter
put his things into a bag. She
and David didn't see that the counter
was wet.

David left the supermarket
and started home.

The sun felt good on his back,
and he began to whistle.

But the wet bottom of the bag
began to fall apart.

David was whistling so hard that
he didn't see something wrapped
in brown paper fall to the ground.

He moved the bag he was carrying
from one arm to another and walked on.

Then David saw
a frisky black and white dog
playing in front of a red house.
He stopped to play with it.
    And he didn't see *another* something
wrapped in brown paper fall
to the ground!

David went by the school
where he would be going in September.
This time he *did* see
something wrapped in brown paper
fall from the bag.

"OH!" said David. "This bag
is *wet!*"

"And it has a big *hole* in it!

"AND WHERE'S ALL THE MEAT
I GOT AT THE SUPERMARKET?!"

JUST IN TIME David picked up
the last something that had fallen.

There were four dogs
about to eat up all the meat
inside the brown paper!

"Oh!" said David. He turned around
and ran back toward the red house
as fast as he could run.

The four dogs ran behind him
as fast as *they* could run!

David and the four dogs
came to the red house.
In front of the red house were
many, many dogs in a circle.

But in the center of the dogs
David could see a brown wrapping
with one hot dog showing.

"OH MY!" said David. He sat down
with his back against a tree and
tried to think of something to do.

He couldn't think of anything at all.

Then the black and white dog
came out of the house and barked
the loudest barks that David
had ever heard.

And all the other dogs backed away
from the meat.

Then, "Oh my goodness!" said David.
"I still haven't found all the meat!"

He picked up the hot dogs and
ran back toward the supermarket
as fast as he could run.

The dogs ran behind him
as fast as they could run!

David counted four dogs and
eight dogs—twelve dogs altogether!

Near the supermarket David found
more dogs and a brown wrapping
with nothing in it.

There was a very little bit
of hamburger left on the brown paper.

"There's no use in picking *that* up,"
thought David.

He went back to the supermarket
to get some more meat.
The dogs followed him and waited
outside the door.

There were twenty-nine dogs
when David came out of the supermarket.
When he started home, they
followed along behind him. They held
their heads and tails high in the air.

People began to stop and point
at David.

"It's a parade," one little girl
said.

"Yes, it's a parade," a little boy
agreed.

They followed along behind David,
too.

"Go home!" David said to the dogs.

But they still followed him.

"It's *not* a parade," said David
to the children.

But they followed him, too.

David gave up.

There was nothing to do
but walk along
with the children
and the dogs
behind him.

The line grew—and GREW—and *GREW!*

Children saw their dogs in the line,
and parents saw their children.
Everyone followed along.

David could still count
twenty-nine dogs behind him.

There were too many children
for him to count at all!

When David came to the door
of his home he walked right past it
and turned around again.

"How can I go home?" he wondered.
"Mother and Father wouldn't know
what to do with twenty-nine dogs!
And neither would I!"

He headed back toward the supermarket.

On the way he passed
the school again.

The school band had just finished
practicing. They came through
the school doors and saw David.

"What's your name?" asked the leader
of the school band.

"David McCheever," said David.

"We'll help you lead your parade,"
said the boy. "How many dogs are there?"

"Twenty-nine," said David proudly.

Then the band followed along

behind David, too, with the big
bass drum in the lead.

"OH MY," said David. The band
began to play a marching song
and everyone walked a little faster.

"What's the parade for?" asked
a man.

"It's David McCheever's twenty-nine
dogs," replied the band leader.

"OH," said the man. He followed
along, too.

A policeman
on a motorcycle asked,

"What's going on here?"

"It's David McCheever's twenty-nine
dogs," said the band leader.

"Oh," said the policeman. He
started his motorcycle
and led the parade.

More and more people
joined the parade.

Stores and offices were closed,
and everyone came to march
with David McCheever and
his twenty-nine dogs.

"It's David McCheever's
twenty-nine dogs," they said
to one another.

David was having a good time.

He marched along happily,

whistling the tunes that the band played.

Everyone else began to whistle, too.

David felt very important.

A man came by with a camera
and took pictures of the parade.

"David McCheever's twenty-nine dogs,"
he said to himself. "It will be
in tomorrow's paper."

The parade became more and more fun.
David hoped it would never stop.

Then suddenly a black cat
crossed the street
right in front of the parade.

AND

ALL

SORTS

OF THINGS

BEGAN

TO HAPPEN!

Away went David McCheever's
dogs after the cat!

And away went all the children
after David McCheever's dogs!

And away went the parents
after the children
who went after the dogs
who went after the cat!

All of them
began to run
through the streets
of the city.
    They ran past
the supermarket.
    They ran past
the school.
    They kept
on running
until the black cat
climbed a tree.

Then the children took their dogs,
and the parents took their children,
and everyone went home.

David was left all alone.

There was no more policeman

on a motorcycle.

There was no more big bass drum.

There was no more school band.

There were no more children

and no more dogs.

There was no more ANYONE!

David felt lonely. Then
he saw the frisky black and white dog
standing there next to him.

"I guess I'd better take you home,"
David said. He began to walk
toward the red house.

The dog followed along.

"A fine parade, David McCheever,"
said the man who answered the door
at the red house. "I haven't ever
had such a good time before."

David stopped short. No one in town
had ever known his name before
without being told what it was!

He thought about this
while he was walking home.

"Hello, David McCheever," said
a woman he met on the way. "We
enjoyed your parade."

"Hi, David," said a boy
with a big ice cream cone. "Your parade
was great!"

"Hello," David said to the people
he passed. He smiled and walked along
faster. After a while he began
to whistle again.

"Everyone knows me," he thought
to himself, "and pretty soon
I am going to know *them*, too!"

Then he began to run home
as fast as he could to tell
his parents all about it.

"Everybody knows it was *my* parade,"
he thought to himself, and he ran even
faster.

"Hi, David," his mother said
when he opened the door. "You
missed a wonderful parade!"

"Did you see all the dogs and
the children marching through the city?"
asked his father.

"It was a great parade," said the boy
who was delivering the newspapers.

Then everyone began to talk all at once
about the parade.

47

But David was so out of breath
from running home to tell all about it
that he couldn't say anything at all!